THE OFFICIAL
EVERTON ANNUAL

2010

Written by Darren Griffiths,
Adam Clark and Matthew Gamble

A Grange Publication

© 2009. Published by Grange Communications Ltd., Edinburgh, under licence from Everton Football Club. Printed in the EU.

Every effort has been made to ensure the accuracy of information within this publication but the publishers cannot be held responsible for any errors or omissions. Views expressed are those of the author and do not necessarily represent those of the publishers or the football club. All rights reserved.

Photographs © Action Images and Press Association Images.

ISBN 978-1-906211-78-3

£6.99

THE CONTENTS

For the third time in five years he was voted as the League Managers Association 'Manager of the Year'.

DAVID MOYES

"I think it meant a lot to Everton supporters to be at Wembley. They were great and they never gave up on us."

David Moyes was a very proud man on May 30th 2009 when he led his Everton team out at Wembley for the FA Cup final against Chelsea.

He became the first Blues manager since Joe Royle in 1995 to take an Everton team to the cup final and although the afternoon ended in defeat, Moyes accepted the outcome with dignity.

"They were worthy winners," he said. "It's really hard to win things in England but we deserved to be in the final because we beat some big teams to get there."

"Playing Chelsea was just a hurdle too much for us. They were the better team but I'm actually very proud of the players for the efforts they have put in all year."

Moyes has never been one for making excuses but there was no doubt that dreadful injuries to key players had made Everton's task all the more difficult.

"If Chelsea had gone into the game without Lampard, Drogba and John Terry, it would have given us a big lift," he said. "We went in without Yakubu, Arteta and Jagielka."

Even without those three players it was still a gallant effort by Everton and it was a performance that the traveling supporters could be proud of.

"I think it meant a lot to Everton supporters to be at Wembley," Moyes added. "They were great and they never gave up on us."

The Blues may have lost at Wembley but David Moyes didn't end the season empty-handed. For the third time in five years he was voted as the League Managers Association 'Manager of the Year' – a remarkable achievement.

"It's always nice to be recognised by your fellow managers and I'm very proud to have won it three times but, as I have said many times before, I would rather win team awards," he said. "I see this as an award for the club as much as myself and it's a reflection on how well the players have done again."

"We started losing players at Christmas time, then lost Mikel and Victor Anichebe in February so to finish fifth and reach a cup final is a great achievement. We look like we can compete consistently at the top end now."

Certainly, Everton are now considered to be one of the big teams capable of battling for honours every season...and that wasn't the case when David Moyes first became manager back in 2002.

"When I first took over, we finished seventh in my first full season," he recalled. "A lot was made of it but the next year we couldn't do it and people used to say it was one good year followed by a bad one."

"Well Everton look as if we have got rid of that now and a lot of what we have done is built on old fashioned values."

FA CUP FINAL

The Toffees scored the quickest FA Cup final goal of all time at just 25 seconds!

The FA Cup Final is one of the most famous football occasions in the world. Fans of all ages can recall their own personal favourite cup final matches and moments and it's watched by billions worldwide.

All Evertonians were fervently hoping that 2009 was going to be their year. After all, the team had beaten Liverpool, Aston Villa and Manchester United to get to the final.

It was a typically glorious May afternoon and Wembley Stadium was basking in sunshine as Everton kicked off... but few could have expected what would happen in the opening half a minute.

The Toffees scored the quickest FA Cup Final goal of all time when Louis Saha smashed an unstoppable shot past Chelsea keeper Petr Cech. It was timed at just 25 seconds and the Evertonians celebrated wildly!

Sadly, it just wasn't to be and the mega-rich Londoners fought back to equalise before half-time thanks to a header from Didier Drogba.

It was all to play for in the second period but despite Saha coming close again, it was Chelsea who scored the deciding goal through England midfield star Frank Lampard – 29 years after his dad had scored an FA Cup semi-final winner against Everton for West Ham United!

So, it was John Terry and not Phil Neville who lifted the FA Cup trophy at the end of the afternoon but all Evertonians left Wembley feeling very proud of their team. They'd given everything they had and it had been a memorable day...

A memorable day...

The Everton players have always been aware of their community responsibilities and as you can see from these pictures they enjoy nothing more than getting out and about to meet young children.

A personal visit from Louis Saha certainly cheered this young man as he recovered in hospital.

Tim Cahill helps to bring some Christmas cheer to a young boy at Liverpool's Alder Hey Children's Hospital. The players take presents to the youngsters every year and it's a visit that is enjoyed as much by the footballers as it is by the children.

50 years of care
Marie Curie Hospice
Liverpool

Steven Pienaar and Tim Howard have won plenty of international caps between them but it's doubtful whether or not they've ever worn large yellow top hats! But they were happy to do so at Finch Farm to help celebrate the Marie Curie Cancer Charity's 50th anniversary.

Phil Jagielka took time out during the busy spring football schedule to take some Easter eggs to a children's hospice.

Whether it's a hospital visit, a coaching session at a local sports centre or a trip to Goodison Park to work with schoolchildren at the Everton Study Centre, the players are happy to help out.

The Premier League Creating Chances initiative enables top stars to get out and about and contribute to worthwhile causes. This is Leighton Baines at a Liverpool Sports Centre with a group of youngsters who had enjoyed a coaching session.

Jags again - this time at Goodison Park. A group of local schoolchildren were learning how to produce a television programme and the Blues defender was a more than willing 'guest' on their show.

SEASON REVIEW 08/09

Everton once again toured the United States of America during the pre-season campaign and although it was another successful trip, doubts were being voiced about whether or not the squad was going to big enough when the Premier League season started in **AUGUST**.

Those worries were confirmed when Everton lost both their opening home fixtures.

With a substitutes bench packed with untried teenagers and Jack Rodwell getting his first ever start, Everton welcomed Paul Ince's Blackburn Rovers to Goodison Park on the first day of the new campaign.

Despite goals from Mikel Arteta and Yakubu, the visitors took all three points with a late goal. History was made that afternoon when

Jose Baxter came on in the second half to become the club's youngest ever first-team player.

Baxter was actually in the starting eleven the following week when Everton went to newly promoted West Brom. It was a much better performance and strikes from Leon Osman and Yakubu gave David Moyes' side a much-needed 2-1 success.

The Yak had made a good start to the season but he then missed a penalty in the next game against Portsmouth at Goodison on a day when just about everything went wrong. The south-coast team outclassed a nervy Everton and although the eventual 3-0 scoreline probably flattered them, few could argue that The Blues deserved to lose.

The first game of **SEPTEMBER**, when Everton went to the Britannia Stadium to face Stoke City, was another dramatic afternoon! There were five goals scored and David Moyes was sent-off after Everton were denied a clear penalty!

Tim Cahill made his first appearance of the season after recovering from injury and it was him who scored the winning goal after Stoke had pulled level from being two goals behind. Yakubu, again, and his Nigerian team-mate Victor Anichebe had given Everton a 2-0 lead but an inability to deal with the remarkable long throws of Rory Delap helped the home team back level before Cahill struck.

YAKUBU!

NEVILLE!

GOAL

The Belgian side Standard Liege were Goodison's next guests for a UEFA Cup 1st Round tie and a 2-2 draw left Everton with a lot to do in the second leg. Yakubu and Segundo Castillo scored for The Toffees.

Incredibly, Everton's first three away games of the season were against the three newly promoted teams and after wins at West Brom and Stoke, it was off to Hull City. It was another 2-2 draw – but this time it was Everton who came from 2-0 down, thanks to goals from Cahill and Osman.

September was proving to be a very tricky month and the mood didn't get any better when Everton were dumped out of the Carling Cup by Blackburn Rovers. It was a miserable night in Lancashire as Rovers won a scrappy game 1-0.

Confidence was understandably low ahead of the first Mersey derby of the season – and the game went true to form with Liverpool winning 2-0 at Goodison.

Fernando Torres scored both Liverpool goals, Everton rarely threatened at the other end and Tim Cahill was sent-off.

Everton needed a boost as **OCTOBER** dawned but they didn't get it in Europe when the stiff task of beating Standard Liege in Belgium proved just too much. Phil Jagielka scored his first goal of the season but Everton lost 2-1 to bow out of the UEFA Cup.

The Blues were still looking for their first home win of the campaign when Newcastle United arrived. It started well with Mikel Arteta and Marouane Fellaini giving Everton a 2-0 lead but again it didn't last and the Magpies took a point from a 2-2 draw. The subsequent, and entirely expected, 3-1 loss at Arsenal's Emirates Stadium left Everton in 16th place in the Premier League table. Leon Osman had opened the scoring in London but The Gunners were just too strong.

There was no doubt about it – Everton were suffering. Self-belief was very low and the last thing the team needed was a clash with Manchester United. Sure enough, Darren Fletcher gave the champions a half-time lead but after the break the game changed... and so did Everton's season!

Phil Neville thundered into Cristiano Ronaldo early in the second-half and Goodison was suddenly lifted. It was a fair tackle, even though the referee gave a free-kick, and it inspired Everton. Fellaini headed an equaliser and Yakubu came very close to scoring a winner. The game ended 1-1 but The Toffees took heart from their display.

The last game of **OCTOBER**, against Bolton Wanderers at The Reebok, was no cracker but Everton won it thanks to a stoppage time goal from Fellaini – his third in four games. The tide was turning!

The tide was turning!

The Goodison jinx was finally broken at the seventh attempt when Everton beat Fulham 1-0 on the first day of **NOVEMBER**. Louis Saha, a former Fulham player, was the hero when he headed a second-half goal after coming on as a substitute. It was his first goal for the club since his summer switch from Manchester United.

The Frenchman took his good form into the next game but he left it late before putting West Ham to the sword at Upton Park. The Hammers led until late in the game when, in an amazing turnaround, Everton pinched it with two goals from Saha and one from Joleon Lescott.

That was three wins in succession for a rejuvenated Everton and the Premier League table was making far more pleasant reading with the team now up to 7th position.

The visit of Middlesbrough therefore held no fears for The Toffees but it was a frustrating afternoon and Everton needed a Yakubu goal in the second half to earn a 1-1 draw.

Before last season, Everton had a very good record at Wigan Athletic's JJB Stadium and confidence was high when they made the short trip on a Monday night for a game shown 'live' on television. It was a chance for Everton to show everyone that they were a much-improved team but they fluffed it. It was a very poor display and Wigan thoroughly deserved their 1-0 win.

From Wigan to London next, and a game against Tottenham Hotspur at White Hart Lane. Everton had won on their previous two visits and they did it again this time! Steven Pienaar was the goalscorer but there was bad news after the game when it was revealed that Yakubu had damaged his Achilles sufficiently to rule him out for the rest of the season.

GOAL

PIENAAR!

GOSLING!

The festive month of **DECEMBER** is traditionally a busy one for football and Everton had some tough-looking fixtures ahead of them. The first, at home to Aston Villa, was one of the games of the season.

Steve Sidwell blasted Villa in front after just 35 seconds to stun the home crowd but Joleon Lescott levelled for Everton just before the half-hour mark. It was thrilling end-to-end stuff and it was the visitors who scored next when Ashley Young netted in the 53rd minute. Everton then took charge but despite countless attacks they just couldn't break through. Then, in stoppage time, Lescott hooked home a brilliant goal to send Goodison into ecstasy. The fans were still celebrating when Villa kicked off and sent through Young to score an unbelievable winner with the last kick of the game! Breathtaking!

There was another late goal the following week at Eastlands against Manchester City but thankfully on this occasion it was Tim Cahill who scored it to give Everton a 1-0 win.

Three days before Christmas, big-spending Chelsea came to Goodison and they had John Terry sent-off for a foul on Leon Osman in the first half. They held firm though and another good game ended 0-0.

The Boxing Day trip to Middlesbrough saw Everton break into the top six in the table for the first time this season. Boro proved to be stubborn opponents but not for the first time Everton were indebted to Tim Cahill who scrambled home the only goal of the match.

Sunderland were the opponents at Goodison for the last game of 2008 and after all the previous December drama, the Evertonians were glad of a comfortable 3-0 win. Mikel Arteta scored twice and there was a first-ever club goal for Dan Gosling.

A first-ever club goal for Dan Gosling.

Jack Rodwell was just 16-years-old when he made his debut for Everton in a UEFA Cup tie against AZ Alkmaar.

At the start of this current season he'd turned 18 and was looking to establish himself as a Premier League footballer after playing an important role in a successful Everton season of 2008/2009.

As well as hoping to play even more games this season, Jack was also hoping to retain his place in the England Under-21 set-up. He was a part of the young Three Lions squad that reached the final of the European Under-21 Championships in Sweden in the summer.

So he's really enjoying life at the moment – and he's keen to thank the Everton manager David Moyes for his influence so far.

"The manager has been amazing," he said. "He's a great gaffer to have - he's helped me a lot because I'm young."

"He puts his trust and faith into the youngsters as you've seen over the past years, which is good for me and good for the youngsters coming through at Everton."

That faith in Jack Rodwell's ability is something that's shared by his team-mates. Phil Jagielka was the 2008/09 Everton Player of the Season and he's looking forward to seeing Jack develop even more.

"Jack's a fantastic player," he said. "People keep talking about how much of a prospect he is but he's already a great player now and hopefully he will have a lot more of a part to play in our season next year and we will see where that takes him."

England Under-21 manager, Stuart Pearce, is just as excited by the Birkdale-born teenager.

"The Rodwells of this world look like they can take anything on," beamed Pearce.

"He plays beyond his years. He's quiet but he's strong mentally. All the time he is flourishing more and more."

That Jack has a big future ahead of him is clearly beyond question. But there has been some debate about whether he will be better suited to the midfield area or the defensive zones as he gets older.

Some football pundits have suggested he could be another Rio Ferdinand.

"I have been playing in midfield and I believe that Rio did the same when he was younger and then moved back to centre-half," said Jack.

"I am not sure what will happen with me but I look up to him. I have heard the comparisons and it's brilliant to be compared with such a player as Rio Ferdinand."

"I try to base it on my own game. I do like to play out from the back, so that's probably why they have played me in midfield because I am comfortable on the ball."

Wherever he plays on the field, it's safe to say that there's plenty more to come from Jack Rodwell.

The Rodwells of this world look like they can take anything on!"

WORD SEARCH

FIND THE EVERTON STARS!

```
J Z D L X N M Q P L N H
A Y G N I N I A L L E F
G J A C O B S E N I V W
I W T F F A W R L H I W
E L X Z T D U R R A L N
L T N E O B A O K C L T
K F T R U A O P B T E D
A R A K N I N S G O F R
A Z A E Q N R N M G Y A
F Y I R G E Z T Z A T W
K P P R L S T N M B N O
T R E B B I H S A H A H
```

HOWARD	RODWELL	NEVILLE
PIENAAR	HIBBERT	ARTETA
JACOBSEN	YOBO	SAHA
OSMAN	JAGIELKA	YAKUBU
BAINES	CAHILL	FELLAINI

ANSWERS ON PAGE 61

18

WELCO
TO

Welcome
to Finch

Ev

finc
trainin

we

The indoor
pitch is huge
and is covered
with Astroturf.

This is the
gymnasium
that the players
use to maintain
strength and
fitness.

Everton's state-of-the-art training ground at Finch Farm first opened in October 2007.

Here's an inside look at the magnificent complex that the first-team, the reserves and all the academy teams call 'home'...

INCH FARM

This is the reception area where all the visitors report to when they arrive at Finch Farm.

Finch Farm from the outside.

This is the indoor swimming pool.

The cycling machines are a popular form of fitness equipment.

This is the media theatre where David Moyes conducts his pre-match press conferences.

One of the first-team training pitches.

GREAT KEEPERS

The Toffees have had some very famous number 1s over the years – here's our Top Five Goalies to have played between the sticks at Goodison Park...

In the 2008-09 season, Tim Howard created an Everton Premier League record when he kept 17 clean sheets. Tim had a great season and is the latest fab goalkeeper to play for Everton.

TED SAGAR
1929 - 1953

5

1

TIM HOWARD
2006 -

NIGEL MARTYN
2003 - 2006

2

NEVILLE SOUTHALL
1981 - 1998

3

4

GORDON WEST
1962 - 1973

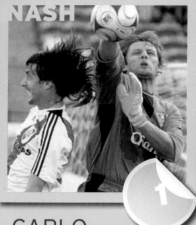

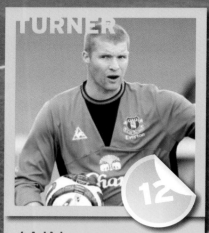

CARLO
NASH
1

Carlo joined Everton on transfer deadline day in September 2008.

The much-travelled goalkeeper brings a wealth of experience to David Moyes' squad.

Beginning his career in non-league football with Rossendale United, Carlo progressed through the Football League, enjoying a successful three-year spell with Stockport County before joining Manchester City.

He went on to play for Middlesbrough and Reading - where he kept a club record 24 clean sheets in one season - before returning to the top flight with Wigan Athletic.

In March 2008, he joined Stoke City on an emergency loan, helping the Potters secure promotion to the Premier League.

He joined Everton on a two-year deal with an option for a further year. Carlo provided back up for Tim Howard, but wasn't able to play a single minute of first-team football in his first season.

IAIN
TURNER
12

Highly-rated goalkeeper Iain arrived at Goodison in January 2003 in a £50,000 deal from Stirling Albion.

He made his Blues debut in a 3-0 friendly win over Bologna in August 2003 but was soon sent on loan to Chester City to gain valuable experience.

A further loan spell at Wycombe followed before a competitive Everton debut as a late replacement for the injured Richard Wright in a 4-1 FA Cup 4th round defeat at Chelsea in February 2006. His Premier League bow came just three days later when Blackburn visited Goodison but the Scot was dismissed for handling outside the area after just eight minutes. He has since had further loan spells at Sheffield Wednesday and Nottingham Forest and remains a regular for Everton's reserve team.

Having been previously capped at Under-16, Under-18 and Under-21 level, Iain finished the 2008/09 campaign with his first Scotland 'B' appearance.

TIM
HOWARD
24

Since joining in the summer of 2006 Tim has made Everton's goalkeeper spot his own.

He arrived from Manchester United, originally on loan, before making a permanent switch in February 2007.

Tim's career began in his native USA where he played for the New York Metrostars (now the New York Red Bulls) before catching Sir Alex Ferguson's eye. In the summer of 2007, he was an instrumental figure for his nation as they beat Mexico 2-1 to win the CONCACAF Gold Cup.

He has continued to be the model of consistency and during the 2008/09 campaign, he beat Neville Southall's Everton Premier League clean-sheet record, keeping 17 in total. He also famously saved two penalties in the FA Cup semi-final shoot-out against his former club Manchester United as Everton triumphed.

PLAYER PROFILES

PLAYER PROFILES

Everton

COLEMAN

HIBBERT

2

SEAMUS
COLEMAN

Seamus is a right-back who has represented the Republic of Ireland at both Under-21 and Under-23 level.

He began his career as a central midfielder before switching to full-back and it was with Sligo Rovers that he first caught David Moyes' eye.

Despite reported interest from Celtic, Birmingham City and Ipswich Town, Seamus opted for Everton and signed a professional contract at the end of the 2009 January transfer window. He linked up with Andy Holden and Alan Stubbs in the Blues' reserve-team squad, where he impressed enough to be named as the first-team's 19th man for February's Premier League trip to Newcastle United.

31

TONY
HIBBERT

Rated by many as the best tackler at the Club, Academy graduate Tony has forged an impressive career with Everton.

Originally a midfield player, the Liverpool-born right-back was a member of the Toffees' 1998 FA Youth Cup winning side. He made his first-team debut under Walter Smith in March 2001 when Everton defeated West Ham 2-0 at Upton Park. Indeed, Tony was tripped inside the Hammers penalty area to earn the spot-kick that led to the first goal.

The popular defender has now played over 200 games for The Blues but at the end of the 2008-09 season he was still chasing that elusive first goal!

JOSEPH
YOBO

Joseph was David Moyes' first Everton signing, joining in the summer of 2002.

The Nigerian's pace and versatility were key factors in the decision to take him from French giants Marseille. He won Everton's Young Player of the Year Award for the 2003/04 season and was again one of the most consistent performers during the 2005/6 campaign. Joseph then played every minute of every Premier League game during 2006/07, matching a top-flight feat last achieved 20 years earlier by Kevin Ratcliffe.

In the past two seasons, Joseph has played a vital role in guiding the Blues to successive fifth-place finishes in the Premier League and played at Wembley in Everton's first FA Cup final appearance for 14 years. He signed a five-year contract extension in June 2009.

LEIGHTON
BAINES

Leighton joined Everton from Wigan Athletic just a few days before the start of the 2007/08 season.

He had been on the Toffees' books as a youngster before making his senior debut for Wigan at the age of 17. He went on to make nearly 150 appearances for the Latics, impressing in the Premier League and becoming a regular for England Under-21s. The 2008/09 campaign was arguably Baines' best yet as he made the left-back position his own with a string of excellent performances, which saw him rewarded with a first ever call up to the senior England international squad. Leighton also netted his first goal for the Blues, curling home a spectacular free-kick at Portsmouth and, of course, netted his penalty-kick at Wembley in the FA Cup semi-final.

6

PHIL
JAGIELKA

Phil joined Everton in the summer of 2007 from Sheffield United, having actually been at Everton's Academy for a period in his early teens before departing Merseyside and progressing through the ranks at the Yorkshire club.

The decision to bring him back is arguably one of the best David Moyes has made. Jags got his first real chance when Joseph Yobo left for the African Cup of Nations in January 2008 and he grasped it with both hands, forging a strong partnership with Joleon Lescott which would continue into the following campaign.

His progress since then has been phenomenal. He was handed his England debut as a substitute in a May 2008 friendly against Trinidad & Tobago and then made his first start against European Champions Spain. He scored the winning penalty in Everton's FA Cup semi-final victory over Manchester United and he was subsequently named Everton Players' Player and the fans Player of the Year for 2008-09.

MIKEL
ARTETA

Skilful and versatile, Mikel Arteta is a firm fans' favourite.

10

Starting out at Barcelona aged 15, Mikel has also played for Paris Saint-Germain, Glasgow Rangers and Real Sociedad. While at the latter, Mikel struggled to hold down a regular first-team place and Everton moved to sign him on loan in January 2005. He was an instant success and the switch was made permanent the following summer.

It proved to be a wise move as the Spaniard earned the Club's Player's Player and the fans Player of the Season awards in his first full campaign.

Mikel carried his rich vein of form into the following season and once again picked up the Player of the Year gong. Continued success has seen him rewarded with Everton's famous number 10 shirt and he was handed the captain's armband for the first time in October 2008. Unfortunately, a knee ligament injury sustained at Newcastle in February 2009 ended the Spaniard's season prematurely and he missed both Wembley dates.

LOUIS
SAHA

Louis Saha made history in May 2009 when he smashed home the quickest-ever FA Cup Final goal! He scored after just 25 seconds against Chelsea at Wembley.

The French international joined Everton from Manchester United in the summer of 2008, bringing with him a splendid goalscoring pedigree at the highest level, having scored consistently for both United and previous club Fulham.

Indeed, Sir Alex Ferguson parted with upwards of £12m to take Saha to Old Trafford from Craven Cottage in 2004.

Earlier in his career Louis played 11 games for Newcastle while on loan from his first club Metz.

Louis' initial Everton campaign may have been an injury-blighted one at times, but he still plundered eight goals, including two goals of the season contenders against West Brom at Goodison and West Ham at Upton Park.

8

PLAYER PROFILES

Everton

TIM
CAHILL

A forceful midfielder with remarkable aerial ability, Tim has firmly established himself as a Goodison hero since joining from Millwall in 2004.

In his last season at the New Den, he made an FA Cup Final appearance – something he would repeat with Everton in 2009. His first season in the Premier League saw him finish as Everton's leading scorer and he won the Player of the Season award.

Once again a key figure during the following campaign, the Australian shot to global fame at the 2006 World Cup, coming off the bench against Japan to score twice and turn a 1-0 deficit into an eventual 3-1 win. He is a 'big-game' player and that fact is underlined by the regularity with which he scores against Liverpool.

He has become an indispensable member of David Moyes' squad and again finished as the Club's leading scorer in 2008/09, matching Marouane Fellaini on nine goals.

17

PHIL
NEVILLE

Following a trophy-laden decade at Manchester United, Phil arrived at Goodison in August 2005.

Having helped his former side to six Premier League titles, three FA Cups, the Champions League and the World Club Cup, David Moyes knew exactly what he would be getting from the England international. For that reason he had no doubts in handing Phil the captain's armband when David Weir departed for Rangers in January 2007.

Using his wealth of experience, the younger of the two Neville brothers has since guided the Blues to successive top five finishes in the Premier League. He has also been one of the Club's most consistent performers in that time, playing mainly at right back or in midfield. The 2008/09 campaign was arguably Phil's best though as he led the Blues back to Wembley, scoring from the spot as Everton beat his former employers on penalties in the semi-final.

18

STEVEN
PIENAAR

A star for the national side of 2010 World Cup hosts South Africa, Steven emerged as one of the hottest talents in the game when he broke through the renowned Academy of Dutch giants Ajax.

Joining Everton on loan from his second club Borussia Dortmund in the summer of 2007, he did enough to earn a permanent switch to the Premier League and went on to play a key role as the Blues reached the 2008/09 FA Cup Final.

Following that impressive loan campaign, a toe injury kept Steven out of the team early in 2008/09 but once he returned he showed how much he'd been missed. He scored one of the goals of the season at Aston Villa in April and was the centre of much of the Toffees' best creative play in the latter part of the campaign.

20

PLAYER PROFILES

OSMAN

LEON OSMAN

Leon has risen through the ranks at Everton and is yet another Academy starlet to make the progression into the first-team.

But Leon's dreams of becoming a professional footballer were almost shattered in 2001 when he suffered a serious knee injury.

That problem kept him out of action for almost a year and he didn't make his first-team debut until he was 21.

A midfielder who combines excellent passing and vision with an eye for goal, he forced his way into David Moyes' first-team plans after impressive loan spells at Carlisle United and Derby County. One of the most popular players at the club, Ossie has since become a first-team regular and enjoyed some of his best form during the 2008/09 campaign, scoring a splendid brace at Fulham on the final day to take his season's tally to seven.

FELLAINI

MAROUANE FELLAINI

Marouane signed for Everton in a transfer deadline-beating switch in August 2008.

In bringing the Standard Liege star to Goodison Park, the Blues broke their transfer record, paying £15m for the player. The powerful midfielder had made 84 appearances for the Belgian champions, scoring 11 times. In 2007, he made his debut for Belgium, and continues to be a regular for his national side.

The summer of 2008 saw him feature at the Beijing Olympics - but he was sent off in the opening game against Brazil!

A player renowned for his physical and aerial presence, 'Felli' became an instant hit with the Goodison faithful thanks to his powerful play, his goals... and his hairstyle! 'Fellaini-wigs' are now a regular part of the Goodison match-day scene!

He also finished an impressive first campaign as joint-leading scorer with nine goals.

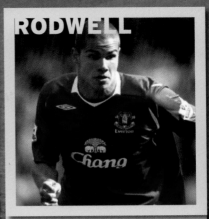

RODWELL

JACK RODWELL

Jack is a record-breaking youngster, having made his full debut against AZ Alkmaar at the age of just 16 years and 284 days to become the youngest Everton player to make an appearance in Europe.

A highly-rated prospect, the Southport-born defender has captained England Under-18s and Under-19s and played in the 2009 European Under-21s Championships.

His Premier League bow came in March 2008 when he appeared as a substitute at Sunderland. He then featured prominently during the pre-season of 2008 and made his first professional start in the Premier League curtain raiser against Blackburn.

The teenager remained in and around the first-team and in February he scored his first senior goal in the 3-1 FA Cup win over Aston Villa.

A few days later he signed a long-term contract with the Toffees and before the season was out he'd played superbly in the FA Cup semi-final win over Manchester United and then scored his first goal for England Under-21s.

PLAYER PROFILES

DAN GOSLING

Dan signed for the Blues during the 2008 January transfer window from Plymouth Argyle, having made his debut for the Pilgrims at the age of just 16.

Right-sided, he can play both in defence and midfield and has been involved with England Under-20s.

His Everton first-team debut came against Middlesbrough on Boxing Day 2008 and he scored his first senior goal just two days later in a 3-0 win over Sunderland. Further cameo appearances followed but it was his 118th-minute winner in an FA Cup fourth round replay against Liverpool at Goodison that truly brought his name to the fore. With the tie heading for penalties, Dan showed remarkable composure for one so young when he curled a lovely shot into the net off the far post.

Dan scored another fine goal, against Manchester City, before the season was out and also made a brief substitute appearance in the FA Cup Final.

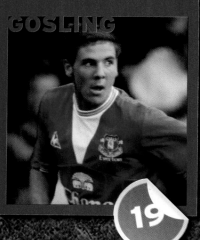

JAMES WALLACE

James joined the Academy set-up aged 13 and was made a full-time scholar in 2008.

The goalscoring midfielder is comfortable in possession and has impressed in his time at Everton.

So much so, that just months after signing a full-time contract with the Everton Academy, Wallace was called into the first-team for a pre-season friendly clash with PSV Eindhoven, making a late substitute appearance.

He went on to train with the first-team for much of the 2008/09 season and was a regular on the substitutes' bench throughout the campaign.

He was also one of the reserve team's most consistent performers.

1878
NIL SATIS NISI OPTIMUM
Everton

PLAYER PROFILES

JAMES
VAUGHAN

James joined Everton's Academy at the tender age of nine - and went on to become a record breaker in the first-team!

A prolific scorer at youth and reserve-team level, he caught the eye of manager David Moyes very early on and aged 16 years and 271 days, a 73rd-minute substitute appearance against Crystal Palace in April 2005 saw him break Joe Royle's record of being the Club's youngest first-team player. He also scored that day to break another record that Wayne Rooney had previously held.

Sadly, James' career has since been plagued by injury and he's had to show every bit of his undoubted strength of character to keep bouncing back. He also showed great courage and ability when he stepped forward to successfully convert a penalty-kick in the FA Cup semi-final against Manchester United.

AYEGBENI
YAKUBU

Ayegbeni Yakubu joined Everton for a then Club record fee of £11.25 million in August 2007.

The Nigerian began his career with Israeli side Maccabi Haifa before moving to Portsmouth in January 2003, where he shot to fame by scoring 29 Premier League goals in just 68 games. Courted by many clubs, Yakubu eventually signed for Middlesbrough for £7.5 million in 2005 and ended the season as the club's top goalscorer with 19 in all competitions.

His Everton career then got off to a flying start when he scored on his debut against Bolton Wanderers. He remained a constant scoring threat throughout the season, managing a career-best haul of 21. It made him the first Toffees player to score more than 20 goals in a season since Peter Beardsley in 1992.

He began the 2008/09 campaign in similar fashion, notching four times in the first five games. Sadly though, his season was ended prematurely when he ruptured his Achilles in November.

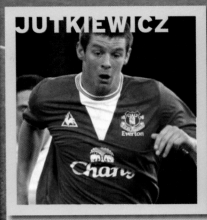

LUKAS
JUTKIEWICZ

Lukas Jutkiewicz arrived at Everton from Swindon in the summer of 2007 after helping the Robins to promotion from League Two.

While at the County Ground, he made regular appearances and scored his first ever senior goal at Walsall's Bescott Stadium in December 2006.

He would total 13 starts, 20 substitute appearances and five goals throughout that promotion campaign.

Lukas made his switch to Everton in the close season and, after being a regular on the bench during the 2007/08 UEFA Cup campaign, was sent on loan to Championship side Plymouth Argyle.

He finally made his Everton debut as a substitute in a 3-0 win over Sunderland at Goodison Park in December 2008. Later in the campaign he joined Huddersfield Town on loan, making seven appearances for the Terriers.

PLAYER PROFILES

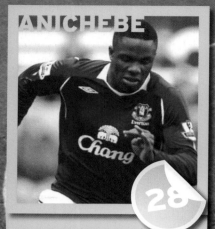

VICTOR
ANICHEBE

Although born in Nigeria, Victor is another product of the Everton Academy.

He progressed to become a regular Under-18s and reserve-team player at the club before graduating to the first-team with a senior debut against Chelsea at Goodison in January 2006. Victor's first senior goal came on the final day of the same season in a 2-2 draw with West Brom.

In April 2006 he signed his first professional contract and the following season he really established himself as a regular in the match-day squad.

He continued his progression in 2007/08, most notably in Europe, scoring four times in the UEFA Cup. He was subsequently voted the Young Player of the Season by supporters.

In March 2008, he made his first appearance for Nigeria, scoring for the Super Eagles Olympic side in a qualifier against South Africa. He later travelled to the Olympics – returning with a silver medal.

Sadly, just as he was showing some top form last season he was on the wrong end of a reckless challenge from Newcastle's Kevin Nolan that left him requiring knee surgery and ended his campaign.

KIERAN
AGARD

The 2008/09 Reserve Player of the Year, Kieran arrived at Everton having started out at Arsenal.

Jet-heeled and with an eye for goal, he scored plenty of goals for the Under-18 side before becoming a regular for the second-team.

In July 2008 he was included on the first-team's summer training trip to Switzerland.

He subsequently made a number of pre-season appearances for the Blues and was an unused substitute in the first two Premier League games of the 2008/09 campaign.

He continued to impress for the reserves and eventually returned to the first-team fold, appearing on the bench towards the end of the season.

JOSE
BAXTER

Jose Baxter has been at Everton since he was just six years old! He left school in May 2008... and was a substitute in the FA Cup Final just a year later!

Born in Liverpool in February 1992, he joined the Everton first-team squad for their tours of Switzerland and America during the 2008/09 pre-season and scored his first goal for the senior team during a friendly at Nottingham Forest in July.

His 77th-minute substitute appearance against Blackburn Rovers on 16 August 2008 saw him become the club's youngest first-team player at just 16 years and 191 days old – breaking a record set by James Vaughan.

The young striker almost scored too but headed narrowly over the crossbar from a tight angle. Seven days later, at West Brom, he became the youngest ever Everton player to start a game. He remained in and around the first-team squad for the remainder of the campaign and was on the bench for the FA Cup final in May.

PLAYER PROFILES

Everton

EVERTON LADIES

The Everton Ladies team continues to go from strength to strength.

Only an agonising 1-0 defeat against Arsenal on the final day of the 2008/09 season saw the Blues miss out on winning the league, but there was still much to be proud of.

Some of the football that the Ladies play is really impressive. In one match last season they thrashed Nottingham Forest 7-0... and they could easily have scored more that day!

Traditionally, Arsenal have been the best team in the league for a number of years and last season was no exception, although Everton, managed by former England international defender, Mo Marley, pushed them all the way.

The Toffees finished second in the league and lost out to the Gunners in the semi-final of the FA Women's Cup.

However, there was some consolation towards the end of the season when Everton recorded the result of the season by beating Arsenal 3-0!

Just how big an achievement it was is summed up by the fact that it was Arsenal's first defeat for 108 matches!

The Everton Ladies team play their home games at Marine FC's ground in Crosby, Merseyside, and the female game is getting bigger and better all the time.

The Blues regularly provide many players for the England international team, including the 2009 Player of the Year Fara Williams, and the manager Mo Marley is very much involved in coaching at the Football Association.

If you're female and you'd like to get involved, why not contact the club and see how you can help out!

DON'T I KNOW YOU?

Phil Jagielka wasn't exactly a stranger when he first joined Everton back in the summer of 2007! He'd played against some of his new Goodison team-mates for his previous club, Sheffield United. Here's some action shots of Jags in opposition to some of the guys who would later become his good friends at Everton!

JAGS V JOLEON
"See you soon pal," said Jagielka. "Yes mate, and we'll be one of the best defensive partnerships in the Premier League," replied Lescott. Probably not true as they shook hands following a Sheffield United v Wolves clash... but that's how it worked out!

JAGS V OSSIE
When Leon Osman was on loan at Derby County he came up against a determined Sheffield United centre-half! The pair are now room-mates at Everton and both claim to have come out on top in this particular battle!

JAGS V YAK
This pair both joined Everton in the summer of 2007 but teaming up at Goodison was the last thing on their minds when they had a right good tussle at Bramall Lane when Yak was at Middlesbrough.

JAGS V VAUGHANY
Jags reckons James Vaughan didn't get a kick in this game... but the Blues young centre-forward thinks otherwise. An early meeting between two men who would later slot home FA Cup semi-final penalties for the

WAS IT A GOAL?

The ball gets played forward and is instantly controlled by an attacking player... Or, the ball gets whipped in from a wide position and an attacking player climbs high above the defenders to head towards goal... Great forward play. But does it end with a goal?

ANSWERS ON PAGE 61

Look at these five pictures and see if you can work out whether or not the ball ended up in the back of the net.

Within seconds of these pictures being taken were the Evertonians cheering like crazy in celebration... or were they holding their heads in their hands after watching a near miss?

PICTURE 1		Yes	No
PICTURE 2		Yes	No
PICTURE 3		Yes	No
PICTURE 4		Yes	No
PICTURE 5		Yes	No

Results 08/09

Everton

SATURDAY, 16 AUGUST 2008	Barclays Premier League	**Everton 2-3 Blackburn Rovers** (Arteta 45+2, Yakubu 64)
SATURDAY, 23 AUGUST 2008	Barclays Premier League	**West Bromwich Albion 1-2 Everton** (Osman 65, Yakubu 76)
SATURDAY, 30 AUGUST 2008	Barclays Premier League	**Everton 0-3 Portsmouth**
SUNDAY, 14 SEPTEMBER 2008	Barclays Premier League	**Stoke City 2-3 Everton** (Yakubu 41, Anichebe 51, Cahill 77)
THURSDAY, 18 SEPTEMBER 2008	UEFA Cup	**Everton 2-2 Standard Liege** (Yakubu 23, Castillo 38)
SUNDAY, 21 SEPTEMBER 2008	Barclays Premier League	**Hull City 2-2 Everton** (Cahill 73, Osman 78)
WEDNESDAY, 24 SEPTEMBER 2008	Carling Cup	**Blackburn Rovers 1-0 Everton**
SATURDAY, 27 SEPTEMBER 2008	Barclays Premier League	**Everton 0-2 Liverpool**
THURSDAY, 02 OCTOBER 2008	UEFA Cup	**Standard Liege 2-1 Everton** (Jagielka 67)
SUNDAY, 05 OCTOBER 2008	Barclays Premier League	**Everton 2-2 Newcastle United** (Arteta (pen) 17, Fellaini 35)
SATURDAY, 18 OCTOBER 2008	Barclays Premier League	**Arsenal 3-1 Everton** (Osman 9)
SATURDAY, 25 OCTOBER 2008	Barclays Premier League	**Everton 1-1 Manchester United** (Fellaini 63)
WEDNESDAY, 29 OCTOBER 2008	Barclays Premier League	**Bolton Wanderers 0-1 Everton** (Fellaini 90)
SATURDAY, 01 NOVEMBER 2008	Barclays Premier League	**Everton 1-0 Fulham** (Saha 87)
SATURDAY, 08 NOVEMBER 2008	Barclays Premier League	**West Ham United 1-3 Everton** (Lescott 83, Saha 85, Saha 87)
SUNDAY, 16 NOVEMBER 2008	Barclays Premier League	**Everton 1-1 Middlesbrough** (Yakubu 65)
MONDAY, 24 NOVEMBER 2008	Barclays Premier League	**Wigan Athletic 1-0 Everton**
SUNDAY, 30 NOVEMBER 2008	Barclays Premier League	**Tottenham Hotspur 0-1 Everton** (Corluka OG 51)
SUNDAY, 07 DECEMBER 2008	Barclays Premier League	**Everton 2-3 Aston Villa** (Lescott 30, Lescott 90+3)
SATURDAY, 13 DECEMBER 2008	Barclays Premier League	**Manchester City 0-1 Everton** (Cahill 90+2)
MONDAY, 22 DECEMBER 2008	Barclays Premier League	**Everton 0-0 Chelsea**
FRIDAY, 26 DECEMBER 2008	Barclays Premier League	**Middlesbrough 0-1 Everton** (Cahill 51)
SUNDAY, 28 DECEMBER 2008	Barclays Premier League	**Everton 3-0 Sunderland** (Arteta 10, Collins OG 27, Gosling 83)
SATURDAY, 03 JANUARY 2009	The FA Cup third round	**Macclesfield Town 0-1 Everton** (Osman 43)
SATURDAY, 10 JANUARY 2009	Barclays Premier League	**Everton 2-0 Hull City** (Fellaini 18, Arteta 45+1)

Results 08/09

Everton

MONDAY, 19 JANUARY 2009	Barclays Premier League	**Liverpool 1-1 Everton** (Cahill 87)
WEDNESDAY, 25 JANUARY 2009	The FA Cup fourth round	**Liverpool 1-1 Everton** (Lescott 27)
WEDNESDAY, 28 JANUARY 2009	Barclays Premier League	**Everton 1-1 Arsenal** (Cahill 61)
SATURDAY, 31 JANUARY 2009	Barclays Premier League	**Manchester United 1-0 Everton**
WEDNESDAY, 04 FEBRUARY 2009	The FA Cup fourth round replay	**Everton 1-0 Liverpool** (Gosling 118)
SATURDAY, 07 FEBRUARY 2009	Barclays Premier League	**Everton 3-0 Bolton Wanderers** (Arteta (pen) 40, Jo 49, Jo (pen) 90+4)
SUNDAY, 15 FEBRUARY 2009	The FA Cup fifth round	**Everton 3-1 Aston Villa** (Rodwell 4, Arteta (pen) 24, Cahill 76)
SUNDAY, 22 FEBRUARY 2009	Barclays Premier League	**Newcastle United 0-0 Everton**
SATURDAY, 28 FEBRUARY 2009	Barclays Premier League	**Everton 2-0 West Bromwich Albion** (Cahill 36, Saha 70)
WEDNESDAY, 04 MARCH 2009	Barclays Premier League	**Blackburn Rovers 0-0 Everton**
SUNDAY, 08 MARCH 2009	The FA Cup sixth round	**Everton 2-1 Middlesbrough** (Fellaini 50, Saha 56)
SATURDAY, 14 MARCH 2009	Barclays Premier League	**Everton 3-1 Stoke City** (Jo 18, Lescott 24, Fellaini 90+1)
SATURDAY, 21 MARCH 2009	Barclays Premier League	**Portsmouth 2-1 Everton** (Baines 4)
SUNDAY, 05 APRIL 2009	Barclays Premier League	**Everton 4-0 Wigan Athletic** (Jo 26, Fellaini 47, Jo 51, Osman 61)
SUNDAY, 12 APRIL 2009	Barclays Premier League	**Aston Villa 3-3 Everton** (Fellaini 19, Cahill 23, Pienaar 53)
SUNDAY, 19 APRIL 2009	The FA Cup Semi-final	**Manchester United 0-0 Everton** (Everton win 4-2 on penalties)
WEDNESDAY, 22 APRIL 2009	Barclays Premier League	**Chelsea 0-0 Everton**
SATURDAY, 25 APRIL 2009	Barclays Premier League	**Everton 1-2 Manchester City** (Gosling 90+4)
SUNDAY, 03 MAY 2009	Barclays Premier League	**Sunderland 0-2 Everton** (Pienaar 48, Fellaini 71)
SATURDAY, 09 MAY 2009	Barclays Premier League	**Everton 0-0 Tottenham Hotspur**
SATURDAY, 16 MAY 2009	Barclays Premier League	**Everton 3-1 West Ham United** (Saha (pen) 38, Yobo 48, Saha 76)
SUNDAY, 24 MAY 2009	Barclays Premier League	**Fulham 0-2 Everton** (Osman 45, Osman 88)
SATURDAY, 30 MAY 2009	The FA Cup Final	**Chelsea 2-1 Everton** (Saha 1)

Q: What other sports do you enjoy?

I've always liked rugby union because my dad played it.

Q: What were you like at school?

I was okay. I did my best but I enjoyed PE more than the other lessons.

Q: What type of music do you like listening to?

I like R&B and hip-hop.

Q: What's your favourite holiday destination?

Dubai.

Q: Do you like watching films?

Yes I do, my all-time favourite is Cool Runnings.

Q: Who's your favourite actor?

Denzel Washington.

Q: ...and actress?

Jessica Alba.

Q: Do you watch much television?

Not really, but when I do I like to watch the soaps!

Q: What's your karaoke song?

No chance! I don't do singing!

Q: Who are the funniest guys in the dressing room?

Bainesy and Jags.

Q: Have you got any hobbies?

I enjoy computer games – the likes of Pro-Evolution.

Q: What was your favourite Christmas present as a child?

I always liked getting a new football kit.

Q: What's your favourite food?

I like Caribbean food. Chicken & rice or curried mutton.

Q: Can you cook?

You must be joking!

Q: What car do you drive?

A Porsche Cayenne.

Q: Did you pass your driving test first time?

No!

Q: Second time?

No!

Q: Third time?

Yes!

Q: Do you enjoy training?

I think every footballer should enjoy training. Of course, it can get tough at times but it's got to be done and if you enjoy it, you get more from it.

Q: How does it feel to run out at Goodison when they play Z-Cars?

It's unbelievable. I made my debut as a substitute but when I had my first start and I actually ran out of the tunnel before the game, Z-Cars made the hairs on the back of my neck stand on end. We played Arsenal and we beat them 1-0 with a very late goal from Andy Johnson.

JAMES VAUGHAN

NAME: James Vaughan
AGE: 21
POSITION: Striker

FOCUS ON 14

Q: Do you like any other sports?

Yes, I like to watch cricket.

Q: What other sportsmen do you most admire?

Roger Federer, the tennis player. He is just so consistent and to keep winning at the top level shows just how great a player he is.

Q: Do you like listening to music?

Yes, occasionally. Kings of Leon are my favourite band.

Q: What things do you watch on television?

I watch Coronation Street and also all the sports news channels.

Q: What were your favourite subjects at school?

I liked PE the best but I also did a bit of Media Studies and I quite liked it.

Q: What's your favourite holiday destination?

Las Vegas.

Q: What's your all-time favourite film?

Kes.

Q: Who's your favourite actor?

Jim Carey.

Q: Who's your favourite actress?

Cameron Diaz.

Q: Have you got a karaoke song?

All the new players have to sing for the rest of the squad when we're on pre-season tour. I sang 'Build Me Up Buttercup'.

Q: Who's the funniest player in the dressing room?

Phil Neville.

Q: Have you got any hobbies?

I enjoy watching DVDs.

Q: What was your favourite Christmas present as a youngster?

A brand new pair of football boots.

Q: What do you like to read?

Autobiographies. I like to read about famous sports stars.

Q: What's your favourite meal?

Fish and boiled potatoes.

Q: Can you cook?

Absolutely not!

Q: What car do you drive?

I am still learning at the moment...

Q: Do you enjoy training?

Yes I do because everything you do on the training ground helps me to prepare for matches.

Q: What's it like to play at Goodison?

I made my Premier League debut at the age of 16 at the start of last season and when I came on as a second-half substitute it was the most incredible feeling. It made me want much more of it.

FOCUS ON

JOSE BAXTER

NAME: Jose Baxter
AGE: 17
POSITION: Midfield/striker

37

1 From which team did Everton sign Phil Jagielka?

2 Which Everton player received the most yellow cards last season?

3 Who was the referee in the 2009 FA Cup final? Mike Riley or Howard Webb?

4 For which country does Marouane Fellaini play?

5 True or false - Everton have never played in the Champions League?

6 To which team did Everton sell Andy Johnson?

7 Without checking a programme - what is James Vaughan's squad number?

8 Which Everton player was signed from Millwall?

9 Who is the youngest - Phil Jagielka or Joleon Lescott?

10 Which team did Everton score three goals against in last season's FA Cup?

11 What have Phil Neville, Louis Saha and Tim Howard got in common?

12 Name the Everton players in the picture below.

ANSWERS ON P61.

JUNIOR QUIZ

SPOT THE DIFFERENCE

CAN YOU SPOT 10 DIFFERENCES IN THESE TWO PICTURES OF JACK RODWELL? **ANSWERS ON P61.**

JANUARY began with an FA Cup 3rd round trip to League Two outfit Macclesfield Town and Everton were pushed all the way by the Cheshire minnows, eventually winning 1-0 thanks to a terrific goal from Leon Osman.

Seven days later, Hull City came to Goodison. Phil Brown's team had already done better than anyone expected but their form had dipped by the time they visited Everton and the Toffees were comfortable 2-0 winners. Marouane Fellaini headed the opening goal early on and then Mikel Arteta blasted home a wonderful free-kick just before half-time to seal the points.

Sadly though, Fellaini was booked and that meant he'd miss the next two games – both against Liverpool!

The first derby of the month was a Premier League clash at Anfield. Liverpool scored first through Steven Gerrard but Everton kept pushing forward and thoroughly deserved the late equaliser by Tim Cahill.

The following week, it was all back to Anfield for an FA Cup 4th round tie. This time it was Everton who scored first when Cahill again found space inside the box and headed goalwards for Joleon Lescott to nod past the keeper. Gerrard scored again to equalise in the second half but it had been a good week for Everton.

The big games were coming thick and fast and next up it was Arsenal at Goodison. The Blues were excellent and looked to have secured a famous win, courtesy of a towering Tim Cahill header, but with the very last attack of the match Dutch winger Robin van Persie thumped a dramatic equaliser for the Gunners.

Undeterred, Everton took their nine-games unbeaten run to Old Trafford to face Manchester United. It was another brave display but it just wasn't to be and a Cristiano Ronaldo penalty gave the eventual champions a narrow victory.

A good week for Everton

GOAL

CAHILL!

JO!

GOAL

Wednesday 4th **FEBRUARY** was a night to remember for all Evertonians. The third meeting with Liverpool in just 16 days ended in a 1-0 win and with it came a passage into Round 5 of the FA Cup. 90 minutes couldn't separate the Mersey rivals and neither could 27 minutes of extra-time but just as a penalty shoot-out was looming, Dan Gosling became an unlikely derby legend with a last-gasp winner!

There was another surprise hero in the very next match. Brazilian striker Jo came on loan from Manchester City during the transfer window and promptly announced his arrival with two goals in a 3-0 success against Bolton Wanderers. The in-form Mikel Arteta scored the other.

Mid-way through the month Everton had another tough FA Cup hurdle to overcome when Aston Villa were the 5th Round visitors to Goodison. But from the early moment that Jack Rodwell scored his first ever senior goal the outcome was rarely in doubt. Villa equalised with a penalty but Arteta also converted a spot-kick and Cahill wrapped it up in the second-half.

The 0-0 draw at Newcastle United was a forgettable football match but Everton still made all the headlines the following day. Mikel Arteta, one of the Players of the Year so far, was stretchered off with ligament damage and his season was over. Later in the game a horrendous Kevin Nolan tackle on Victor Anichebe saw the Blues striker leave the field and his campaign too was finished. Nolan was shown a straight red card but the damage had been done. A very sad day all round.

Struggling West Brom were the last February opponents for Everton and they were competently dispatched thanks to goals from Cahill and Louis Saha.

The first game of **MARCH** was a drab 0-0 draw at Blackburn Rovers. Neither side played particularly well and although Joleon Lescott came close late-on with a volley, a draw was a fair result.

The atmosphere was very different four days later when Middlesbrough arrived at Goodison for an FA Cup quarter-final. The prize was a semi-final appearance at Wembley and Everton surprisingly suffered from first-half nerves. They didn't play well and at the break the dream was dying thanks to a David Wheater goal for the visitors. Thankfully, after a stern interval team-talk, it all came right in the second period. Marouane Fellaini showed his worth in the box once again with a well-timed header to equalise and then Louis Saha also used his head to poach the winner. After 14 years of waiting, Everton were going back to Wembley!

Surprise hero!

41

But there were still Premier League points to be won in the race for Europe and David Moyes' men could afford no slip-ups when they took on Stoke City. It was a return to Goodison for James Beattie but it was to be a losing one for the former Everton centre-forward. Jo, Lescott and Fellaini were each on the scoresheet in a convincing 3-1 win.

And so it was a confident Everton party that made the long trip south to face Portsmouth at Fratton Park.

Leighton Baines had been called into the full England squad and he celebrated by curling a beautiful free-kick into the back of the net after just four minutes. Sadly, that was as good as it got for Everton. Peter Crouch levelled before half-time and the tall striker headed a second goal after the break to secure all three points for Portsmouth.

APRIL began with a Goodison Park goal-feast! Wigan Athletic were in town but they were no match for a really in-form Everton team. The impressive Jo scored two more goals, Fellaini grabbed another and Leon Osman wrapped it all up with a tap-in. It finished 4-0 for The Toffees... and it could have been even more!

There were more goals at Aston Villa the following week but this time they were shared equally. Everton, though, were disappointed after twice leading by two goals.

Cahill and Fellaini gave Everton a great start but big John Carew pulled one back before half-time. Everton kept going though and Pienaar restored the two-goal cushion before James Milner and Gareth Barry earned a point for Villa.

It was a blow for Everton but it was quickly forgotten because it was next stop... Wembley! The FA Cup Semi-final was the most eagerly anticipated match for years and the Everton fans travelled to London in their tens of thousands. They weren't disappointed. A 0-0 scoreline after extra-time meant penalties and although Cahill missed the first for Everton, Tim Howard saved United's first two to give the Toffees the advantage.

Everton won the shoot-out 4-2 with Leighton Baines, Phil Neville, James Vaughan and Phil Jagielka all successfully converting their kicks. The Blues were in the FA Cup Final for the first time since 1995!

More goals!

GOAL

¡FELLAINI!

OSMAN!

GOAL

They stayed in London to prepare for the midweek match at Chelsea (ironically their Cup Final opponents) and they earned a very creditable 0-0 draw.

But the feel-good factor was shattered when Everton lost 2-1 at home to Manchester City in their very next match. The result was poor but the injury to Phil Jagielka that was to force him to miss the rest of the season was heart-breaking. Jags had been brilliant all season and his loss cast a shadow across the whole club.

But there was no time to mope because **MAY** was going to be a very busy month.

Everton were in 6th position in the Premier League as the final few weeks of the season dawned, but they were still more than capable of catching Aston Villa and finishing even higher.

An excellent 2-0 victory at the Stadium of Light against Sunderland was just what was needed as the Club began to recover from the shock of losing Jagielka so close to the Cup final.

Steven Pienaar scored another fine goal and Marouane Fellaini was yet again in the right place at the right time to bring three valuable points back from Wearside.

Tottenham Hotspur had been steadily improving since Harry Redknapp had taken over and their visit to Goodison was eagerly anticipated. Two in-form teams together promised much... but delivered very little!
A goalless scoreline just about summed it all up.

But it was another point and with Villa faltering, Everton had everything to play for. The last home match of the 2008-09 season was against West Ham United and, just like the earlier fixture at Upton Park, it ended in a 3-1 win for Everton.

Another coincidence was provided by Louis Saha who repeated his November trick of putting two goals past The Hammers! The other Everton goal was a first of the season for Joseph Yobo.

The final match of a dramatic campaign came at a ground where Everton hadn't won since 1966! The legendary Alan Ball was the Blues last player to register a winning goal at Fulham's Craven Cottage... but all that was about to change. Leon Osman was the hero in the London sunshine, scoring twice in a 2-0 win.

It had been a fine end to the season and Everton had secured 5th place in the table for the second year in succession.

All that was left now was the small matter of an FA Cup Final...!

Just what we needed!

An Everton quiz that you might need help with!

1 Which three former Everton players played for Hull City in the Premier League last season?

2 Which defender scored 14 goals for Everton when we won the Championship in 1984-85?

3 Which international player was sent-off last season after a bad foul on Leon Osman?

4 This former Everton centre-forward scored goals last season for both Hereford United and Shrewsbury Town. Who is he?

5 Another ex-Everton striker, James Beattie, has played for three teams that begin with the letter 'S' – name them.

6 Who scored Everton's first cup goal of last season?

7 Who was the Everton manager who first brought Duncan Ferguson to the club?

8 Before the 2009 FA Cup semi-final against Manchester United, against which team did Everton play their previous match at Wembley?

9 Think back to last season again. Who was the first Everton player to score two goals in one match – and who was it against?

10 Which club links the following current and former Everton stars – Marcus Bent, David Unsworth, Kevin Kilbane and Leighton Baines.

11 Who is the former Everton player, who later managed in the Premier League, in the picture below?

12 With which did club did David Moyes play his last match as a professional footballer?

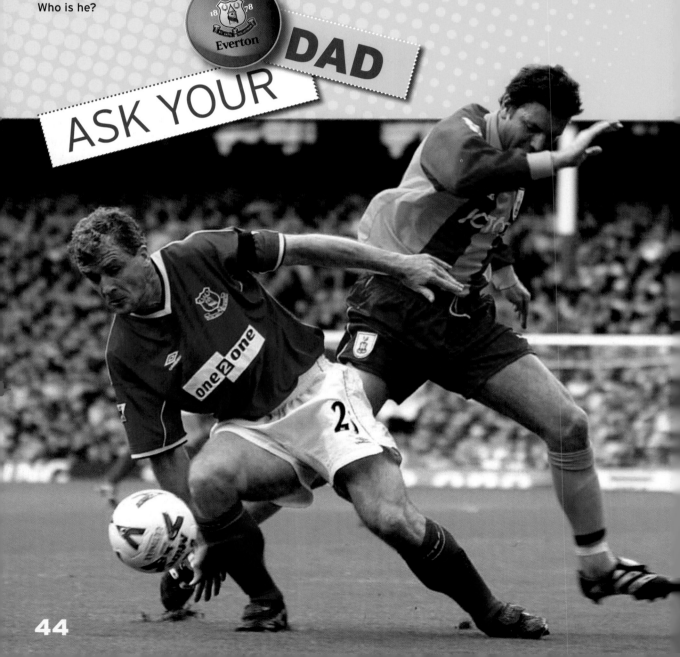

ASK YOUR **DAD**

44

EVERTON TV

evertonfc.com/evertonTV

evertonTV is the Club's online television channel that provides up-to-the-minute news, match highlights and behind-the-scenes footage and features to the Everton supporters all over the world.

We have a dedicated team of camera operators and reporters who work closely with the Everton players to make sure that the breaking-news and post-match reaction is available first on evertonTV for the subscribers who live as far afield as the USA, Asia and Australia!

But news is only a part of the superb package that evertonTV offers. Live audio commentary on every single first-team game is also available, and so are extended television highlights after every match. We've also built up an archive of action from the Premier League years that is well worth a look.

Before every game David Moyes conducts a press-conference at Finch Farm and evertonTV is the only media outlet to always show every single one of them in full.

Figures from the Club's illustrious history are also regulars on the channel, as the likes of Howard Kendall, Alex Young and Dave Watson relive their Everton memories.

We also rub shoulders with the stars of the future by featuring the young players from Everton's academy and reserve teams. Indeed, the evertonTV cameras are regulars at reserve games, giving fans a glimpse of the players closest to breaking into David Moyes' first team.

As well as all this, evertonTV enjoys exclusive access at the stadium and the training ground to be able to provide a glimpse at life behind-the-scenes at Everton.

If you want to enjoy all this and more, you can subscribe to evertonTV simply by visiting:

evertonfc.com/evertonTV

FA CUP RUN

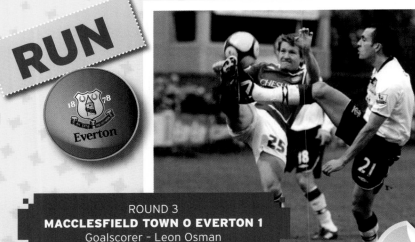

The draw for the 3rd round of the FA Cup is always an occasion to look forward to.

There are sixty-four balls in the large glass bowl at the Football Association headquarters and there are sixty-four sets of supporters eagerly awaiting the identity of their opponents... all of them hoping it's a step towards Wembley and the Final itself!

In January 2009 Everton were drawn away at Macclesfield Town and although we didn't know it at the time, it WAS the first step on the way to the FA Cup Final!

ROUND 3
MACCLESFIELD TOWN 0 EVERTON 1
Goalscorer - Leon Osman

ROUND 4
LIVERPOOL 1 EVERTON 1
Goalscorer - Joleon Lescott

ROUND 4 replay
EVERTON 1 LIVERPOOL 0
Goalscorer - Dan Gosling

5

ROUND 5
EVERTON 3 ASTON VILLA 1
Goalscorers - Jack Rodwell, Mikel Arteta, Tim Cahill

6

ROUND 6
EVERTON 2 MIDDLESBOROUGH 1
Goalscorers - Marouane Fellaini, Louis Saha

SEMI

SEMI-FINAL
EVERTON 0 MANCHESTER UNITED 0
(Everton won 4-2 on penalties)
Goalscorers - Leighton Baines, Phil Neville, James Vaughan, Phil Jagielka

An Everton pre-season tour of the USA has become a regular feature of pre-season under David Moyes.

The manager likes the climate, the facilities and the level of opposition on the other side of the Atlantic and the 2009 schedule was particularly busy. The Toffees spent four days in Seattle, two in Edmonton, Canada and then finished with a week in Salt Lake City.

A few of the lads took a trip to watch the Indy Car Racing in Edmonton.

POSTCARD FROM THE USA

The lads watching the Seattle Sounders baseball side.

David Moyes met some Evertonians in Seattle.

Kasey Keller and Tim Howard face off ahead of the clash with MLS All Stars.

Former Everton midfielder Jimmy Gabriel poses a photo with assistant boss Steve Round.

Phil Neville challenges Freddie Ljungberg whilst the blues take on the MLS All Stars.

Steven Pienaar in action against Argentine side River Plate.

During the trip, Everton lost 1-0 against River Plate and then defeated the MLS All-Stars on penalties and, as you can see from our pictures here, it was a busy but nonetheless enjoyable trip...

The entire Everton team visit director Robert Earl's Italian restaurant while in Salt Lake City.

Joseph Yobo gets a massage from the Club physio.

Jo and Yakubu in Salt Lake City.

There's nothing like
the atmosphere of
a midweek match
at Goodison Park...

GOODISON TOUR

MATCH NIGHT

The semi-final and then the Final of the FA Cup last season gave tens of thousands of Everton supporters the chance they'd waited 14 years for!

Not since the 1995 Charity Shield had Everton played at Wembley and now that they had an opportunity to travel back there again to watch their beloved team, the Toffees were determined to enjoy themselves...

WEMBLEY FANS

PHIL NEVILLE

Q: What was the first ever team you played for?

It was a Sunday League team called Bury Juniors. My first professional team, of course, was Manchester United.

Q: What position did you play when you were at school?

I was a left winger believe it or not!

Q: What about cricket – how far did you go at that sport?

I really enjoyed cricket and I was fortunate enough to captain England Under 15s. I played for Lancashire County Cricket Club and was the youngest ever player to appear for their 2nd XI.

Q: How old were you when you first signed for Man United?

I was 11 years of age when I first started training at United.

Q: Who else was in the youth team with you?

Paul Scholes, Nicky Butt, David Beckham, Keith Gillespie, Robbie Savage… and my brother.

Q: When did you make your first team debut?

It was against Wrexham in an FA Cup tie at Old Trafford. I was 18-years old.

Q: What was Sir Alex Ferguson like with all the young players?

He was like a father to us all. He knew exactly how to treat young players and he used us correctly and at the right times in the first-team. He really looked after us.

Q: What was your first impression of David Moyes?

I was very impressed with the manager from the moment I met him. I could tell that he was absolutely determined to bring success to Everton and he was so thorough and enthusiastic in everything he said. He shared my ambition and that was important.

Q: What do you recall of your Everton debut?

It was a European Champions League game against Villarreal at Goodison Park. The atmosphere was incredible and I remember thinking 'this is the club for me'. The crowd were so good that it felt like my first game ever… and not just my Everton debut!

Q: How proud were you to wear the captain's armband for the first time at Everton?

I was a very proud man. I was proud for myself and my family because I know all about Everton's history and I was aware of just how many great men and wonderful players had been captain of this club.

Q: Were you nervous taking an FA Cup Semi-final penalty?

No I wasn't. Which was a bit strange I suppose because it was the first penalty I had taken in a game since I was 11-years old… and I'd missed that one!

You aspire to captain a team at Wembley in an FA Cup Final and I was a very proud man.

Q: What was it like to walk out as captain at Wembley for the FA Cup Final?

It was a dream come true. You aspire to captain a team at Wembley in an FA Cup Final and, again, I was a very proud man.

Q: When did you make your England debut?

I was 18-years old and England played China in Beijing in May 1996. Gazza was in the team and so were the likes of Alan Shearer, Tony Adams, Darren Anderton and my brother, Gary. We won 3-0.

Q: What was it like playing at Wembley for your country?

I would think that every schoolboy who wants to be a footballer has thought about playing for his country and I was no different. It was a terrific experience to finally wear the Three Lions on my chest at Wembley.

Q: Who did you enjoy playing alongside for England?

Paul Gascoigne. Gazza was a genius, simple as that. The things he could do with a football had to be seen to be believed.

The Everton Tigers team was founded as recently as 2007 and they enjoyed a splendid second successful season in the British Basketball League in 2008-09.

They claimed their first piece of silverware with the BBL Cup when they thrashed Plymouth Raiders 103-49 in a one-sided final at Birmingham's National Indoor Arena in January but lost out to Newcastle Eagles in the other three competitions.

Their campaign ended in agony with a desperately unlucky 87-84 BBL Championship Play-off Final defeat to the Eagles in May.

The Head Coach, Tony Garbelotto, was pleased with the season but he admitted that it could have been even better.

"Big strides have been made both on and off the court this season but I'm disappointed we didn't win more than one trophy," he said.

"We came close but some things let us down. With so many back to back games in this league, the age of our squad was too high and we weren't able to keep playing with the same energy and intensity."

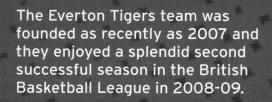

EVERTON TIGERS

"Hopefully we've made the football club proud to be associated with us."

'We're going to have to make changes to the squad and I'm confident we'll put a team together to challenge for all the trophies."

The Tigers at least had some more consolation when star player Andre Smith, a 24-year-old from Minnesota in the USA, finished right at the top of the league's points scoring charts with a stunning average of 26.5 per game.

Smith missed the Play-off final after heading back to America because of a family illness and he was sorely missed.

The Tigers went into the last quarter trailing by 18 points but a heroic performance from skipper Richard Midgley threatened a remarkable comeback.

The Great Britain international helped himself to a record-breaking 36 points in the match.

"We showed great heart and I couldn't question the effort or desire but we couldn't replicate the performance we put in against Leicester in the semi-final," Garbelotto said.

"Newcastle were pretty awesome in the first quarter and built up a massive lead. We chipped away at that and to lose by such a small margin was tough to take. Richard Midgley was unbelievable. He was the best player on the floor."

"Looking at the bigger picture, I think the club has got to be happy with how the season has gone."

"We've really pushed the Tigers out there and started to get ourselves in the sporting minds of the Merseyside public. Hopefully we've made the Football Club proud to be associated with us."

A CAREER IN PICTURES

TIM HOWARD

Tim Howard was born in New Jersey and made his professional football debut for the New York Metrostars in the MLS. He impressed very quickly and made his international debut for the USA in 2002. Before long he was on his way to Manchester United for a reported fee of $4m.

After three seasons at Old Trafford, Tim made the switch to Goodison Park... and he hasn't looked back since!

Signing for Manchester United...

2

...and playing in the 2004 FA Cup Final against Millwall

Howard of United saves from Rooney of Everton!

3

Tim makes a brave save in the 2009 FA Cup Final against Chelsea

Tim is a full USA international and is pictured here with his team-mates before a 2010 World Cup qualifier against El Salvador

4

5

A great save from Rio Ferdinand's penalty in the 2009 FA Cup semi-final

6

In 2006, Tim signs for Everton

7

EVERTON BRANDED GAMES

EVERTON FOOTBALL MANAGER gives you the chance to build an Everton team and go in search of major honours. Starting at the bottom of the football ladder, build a squad from an extensive list of Blues players past and present and begin climbing the leagues, increasing your fanbase and, ultimately, the contents of your trophy cabinet.

The higher you climb, the more Everton legends you can unlock. Heroes of the past like Dixie Dean and Alan Ball are all part of the game as are current stars like Phil Jagielka, Tim Cahill and Mikel Arteta. How they all fit together is up to you!

Have you got what it takes to guide Everton to glory? Get Everton Football Manager and other exciting Everton-branded games for your mobile - for just £3! Visit **evertonfc.com/mobile.**

TEXT ALERTS
Stay in touch with all the goings-on at Goodison wherever you are. Get the latest news, teamsheets, scores and match updates straight to your mobile.

WALLPAPERS
Bored of your mobile? Why not show your true colours with an Everton wallpaper. Choose from match action pictures, Blues legends, official Club crests and much, much more.

ANIMATIONS
Have your Goodison heroes celebrating in 3D on your mobile! Choose from Jags, Fellaini, Cahill, Dixie, Sharpy and more...

VIDEOS
Get the latest Everton highlights straight to your mobile. Download your favourite goals, interviews and classic match highlights to keep in your pocket!

CUSTOMISED SHIRTS
Ever dreamed of seeing your name on the back of Everton's famous royal blue jersey? Choose your own name and number and impress your mates with a personalised home kit wallpaper.

RINGTONES
With our blood-pumping Everton chants, real tones, polyphonics and memorable commentaries, you'll want your phone to ring all day long!

REVERSE AUCTION
Win fantastic prizes and unique opportunities to meet your heroes - for pennies! With Reverse Auction the lowest unique bid wins big.

Go to evertonbid.com to see what's on offer.

P18
WORDSEARCH

```
J Z D L X N M Q P L N H
A Y G N I N I A L L E F
G J A C O B S E N I V W
I W T F F A W R L H I W
E L X Z T D U R R A L N
L T N E O B A O K C L T
K F T R U A O P B T E D
A R A K N I N S G O F R
A Z A E Q N R N M G Y A
F Y I R G E Z T Z A T W
K P P R L S T N M B N O
T R E B B I H S A H A H
```

P33
WAS IT A GOAL?

1) N, 2) Y, 3) N, 4) Y, 5) Y

P39
SPOT THE DIFFERENCE

P38
JUNIOR QUIZ

1) Sheffield United
2) Marouane Fellaini
3) Howard Webb
4) Belgium
5) False, we played in 2005-06
6) Fulham
7) 14
8) Tim Cahill
9) Phil Jagielka – by one day!
10) Aston Villa
11) They were all signed from Manchester United
12) Phil Neville, Jo, Tim Cahill and Leon Osman

P44
ASK YOUR DAD

1) Kevin Kilbane, Nick Barmby, Anthony Gardner
2) Derek Mountfield
3) John Terry
4) Nick Chadwick
5) Southampton, Sheffield United, Stoke City
6) Leon Osman
7) Mike Walker
8) Blackburn Rovers in the 1995 Charity Shield
9) Louis Saha v West Ham at Upton Park
10) Wigan Athletic
11) Mark Hughes
12) Preston

QUIZ ANSWERS

Everton